For Laurel and Shanti,
with much love
from Reeve

❦

For Paul, Louisa,
and William,
with love, Cathie

Text copyright © 1998 by Reeve Lindbergh
Illustrations copyright © 1998 by Cathie Felstead

All rights reserved.
First U.S. edition 1998

Library of Congress
Cataloging-in-Publication Data
Lindbergh, Reeve.
The circle of days / Reeve Lindbergh ; illustrated by
Cathie Felstead.—1st U.S. ed.
p. cm.
"From Canticle of the sun, by Saint Francis of Assisi."
Summary: Rhyming text gives praise and thanks
for all of creation, including wind and sun,
plants and animals, desert, rocks, and sea.
ISBN 0-7636-0357-0
1. Children—Prayer-books and devotions—English.
2. Nature—Religious aspects—Juvenile literature.
[1. Prayer books and devotions. 2. Nature—Religious
aspects. 3. Creation.]
I. Felstead, Cathie, ill. II. Francis, of Assisi, Saint,
1182-1226. Cantico di frate sole. III. Title.
BL625.5.L56   1998
242'.7—dc21   96-49848

10 9 8 7 6 5 4 3 2 1

Printed in Italy

This book was typeset in Leawood Book.
The pictures were done in watercolor,
gouache, and collage.

Candlewick Press
2067 Massachusetts Avenue
Cambridge, Massachusetts 02140

Reeve Lindbergh

The Circle of Days

From *Canticle of the Sun* by
Saint Francis of Assisi

Saint Francis of Assisi (1182–1226) lived in Italy, where he founded the Franciscan order of monks. He is one of the world's best-loved saints, known for his devotion to nature, especially animals and birds. His *Canticle of the Sun*, written in 1225, has been translated into many languages and has been adapted in poetry and song throughout the centuries, as a hymn of praise.

illustrated by

Cathie Felstead

CANDLEWICK PRESS
CAMBRIDGE, MASSACHUSETTS

Lord, we offer thanks and praise
For the circle of our days.
Praise for radiant brother sun,
Who makes the hours around us run.

For sister moon, and for the stars,

Brilliant, precious, always ours.

Praise for brothers wind and air,

Serene or cloudy, foul or fair.

  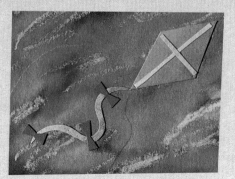

For sister water, clear and chaste,

Useful, humble, good to taste.

For fire, our brother, strong and bright,

Whose joy illuminates the night.

Praise for our sister, mother earth,

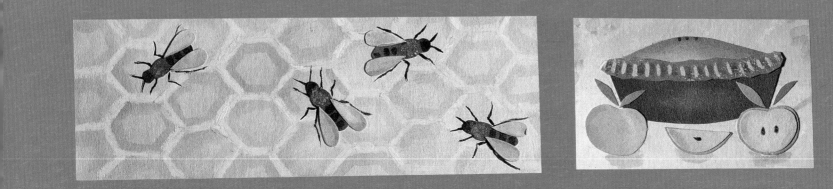

Who cares for each of us from birth.

For all her children, fierce or mild,

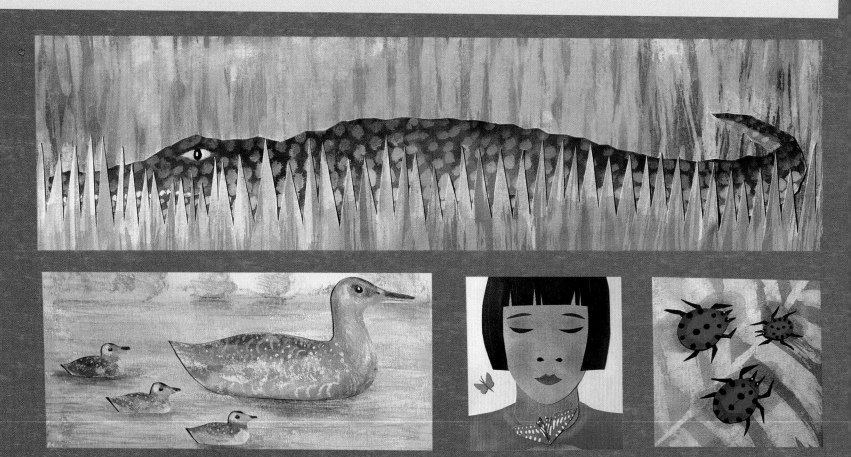

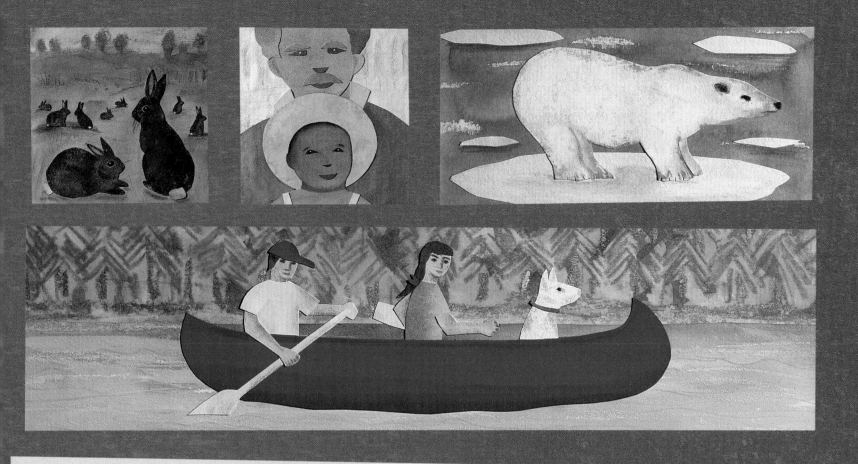

For sister, brother, parent, child.

For creatures wild, and creatures tame,

For hunter, hunted, both the same.

For brother sleep, and sister death,

Who tend the borders of our breath.

For desert, orchard, rock, and tree,

For forest, meadow, mountain, sea,

For fruit and flower, plant and bush,

For morning robin, evening thrush.

For all your gifts, of every kind,
We offer praise with quiet mind.
Be with us, Lord, and guide our ways
Around the circle of our days.